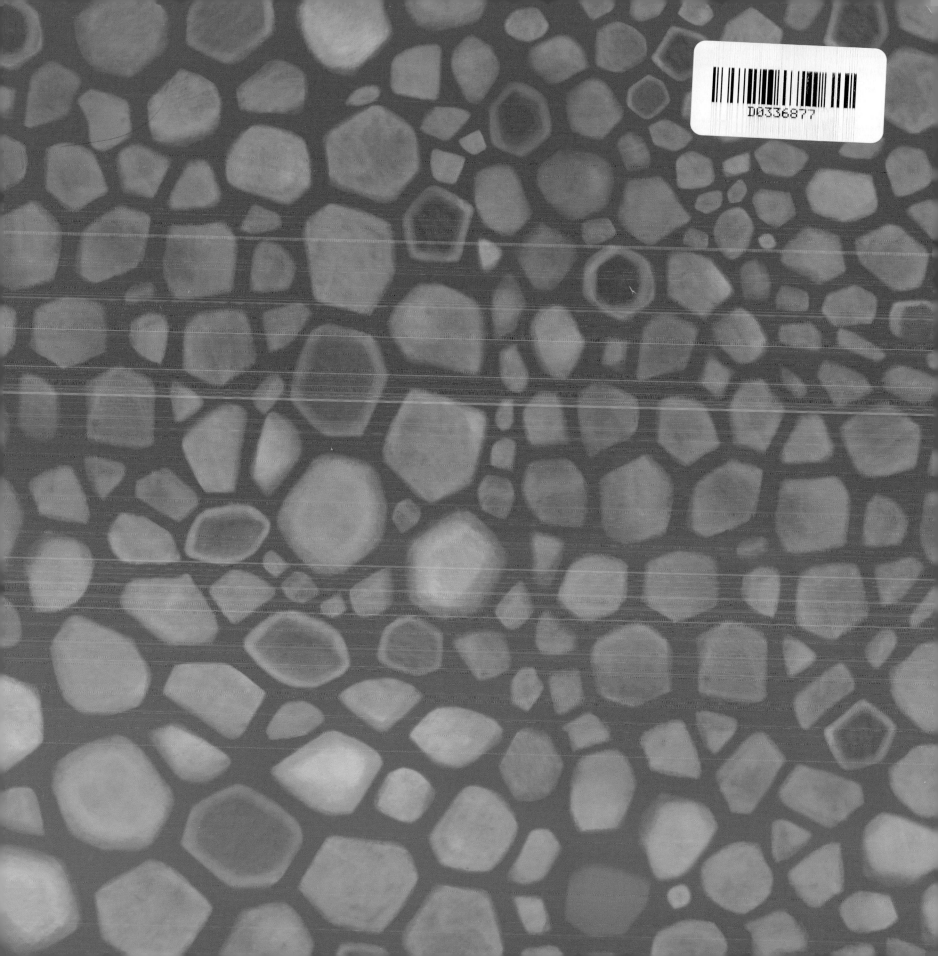

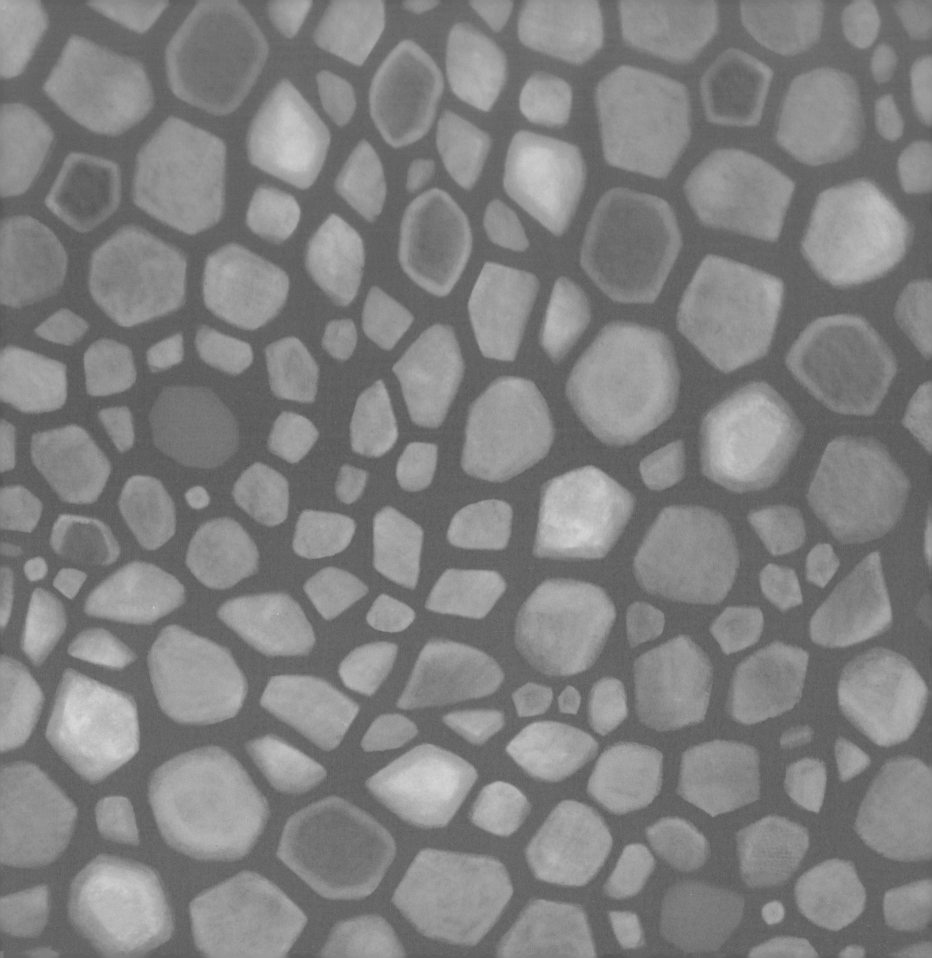

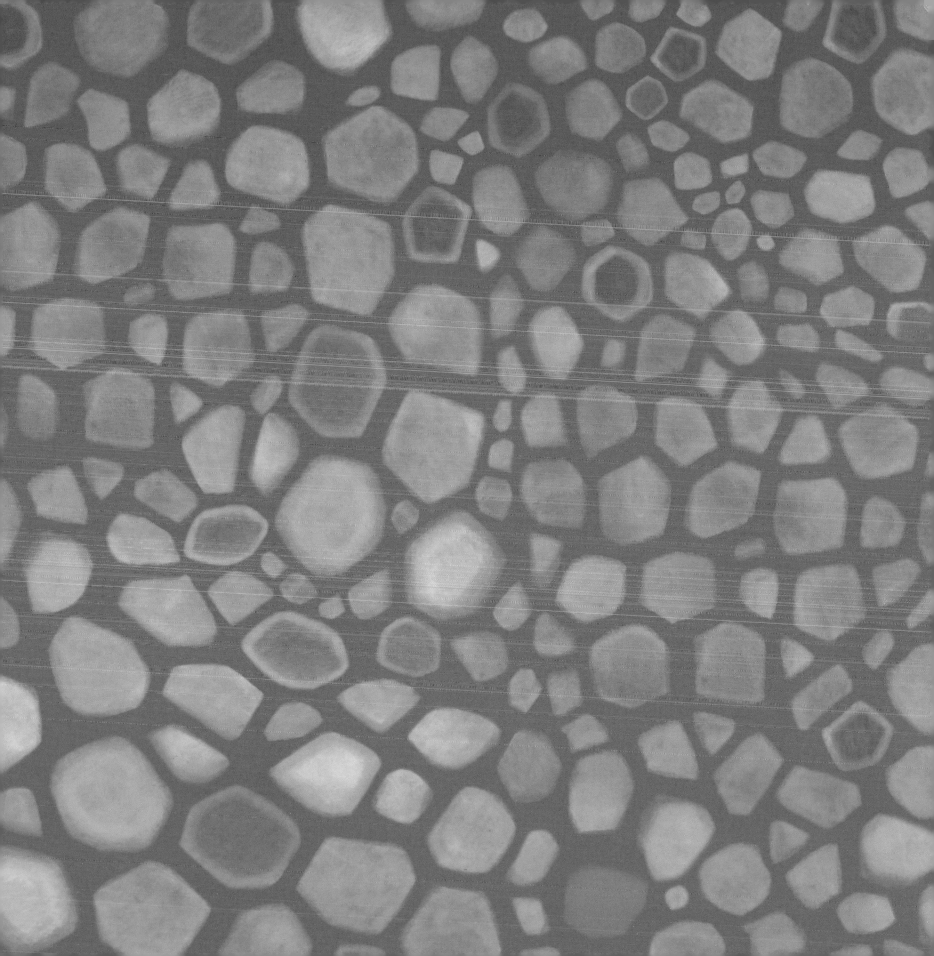

A TEMPLAR BOOK

This book is based on the episode *The Crevice* from the TV series *Gigantosaurus*™.
Screenplay by Franck Salomé, Nicholas Sedel and Fernando Worcel.
The TV series *Gigantosaurus*™ is created and produced by Cyber Group Studios.
Based on the original characters created by Jonny Duddle in the book *Gigantosaurus*,
first published by Templar Books in 2014.

First published in the UK in 2021 by Templar Books,
an imprint of Bonnier Books UK,
The Plaza, 535 King's Road, London, SW10 0SZ
Owned by Bonnier Books,
Sveavägen 56, Stockholm, Sweden
www.templarco.co.uk
www.bonnierbooks.co.uk

1 3 5 7 9 10 8 6 4 2

ISBN 978-1-78741-700-7

Adapted by Mandy Archer
Edited by Lydia Watson and Carly Blake
Designed by Kate Wakeham
Additional design by Adam Allori
Production by: Ché Creasey

Printed in China

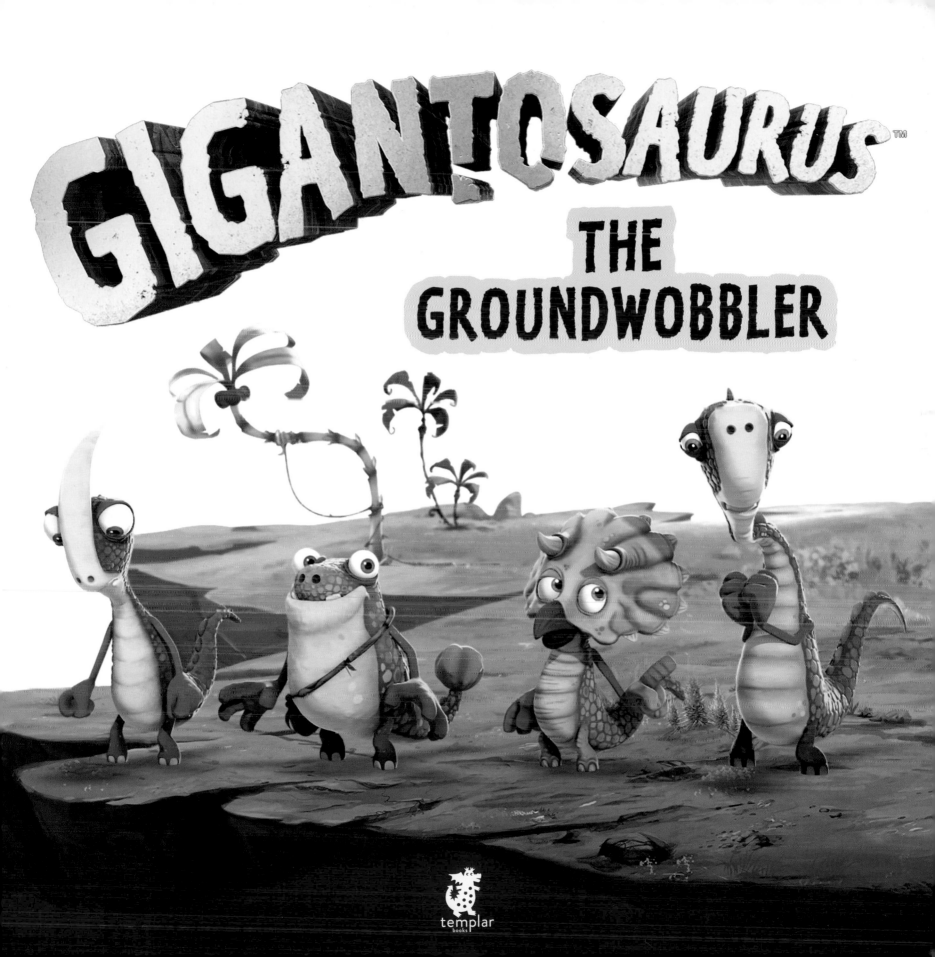

The hot spring next to the volcano was one of the little dinosaurs' favourite places to relax.

Bill was sunbathing by a mud pool, while Mazu and Tiny watched the geysers shoot water up into the air.

But instead of relaxing, Rocky was having fun jumping INTO a geyser. As it erupted, it blasted him high above the treetops – knocking Archie out of his tree!

Poor Archie flapped his wings frantically, but he had never been a good flier.

Sorry, Archie!

With a CRASH and a SPLASH, Archie fell into a mud pool. The noise sent Bill into a panic – Gigantosaurus usually came for his bath around this time!

"Don't worry, it's just Archie," chuckled Tiny.

"I can stay on the lookout for Giganto!" said Archie, clambering out of the mud pool. "But first I need to get back in my tree . . ."

Mazu knew just what to do. She led Archie to a geyser and stirred up the bubbles with her tail. WHOOSH! A jet of water blasted Archie back into the treetops.

Suddenly, the ground began to shake, making Bill even MORE nervous.
"It's just the volcano rumbling, Bill," said Mazu kindly, getting a snack out
of her bag. She knew that food always made Bill feel better.

But the rumbling got louder and louder. Mazu was wrong.
This wasn't the volcano, it was a GROUNDWOBBLER!

"Everyone hold onto me!" shouted Rocky, taking the lead.

Mazu held Rocky's shoulders and Tiny followed behind. Bill brought up the rear, looking around anxiously. Together they marched away from the volcano towards home, singing a song as they went.

Before they had gone far, the ground in front of them split open with a loud CRACK. Mazu pulled Rocky back from the edge just in time, but now the four dinos were stuck.

In front of them was a gaping crevice!

"The wobble's over, Bill! Why are you still shaking?" Tiny asked.

"I'm s-s-scared!" said Bill, trembling. "How are we going to get back to the den?"

"Let's jump across!" suggested Rocky.

Mazu spotted a vine-covered palm tree leaning over the edge of the crevice. It would make the perfect rope swing to get them across the gap.

"I have a very bad feeling about this," groaned Bill.

Rocky went first. He grabbed hold of the vine, took a run up and jumped into the air . . .

Archie walked by just at the wrong moment.
"Hi everyone! Where's Rocky?" he asked – seconds before
the dino landed right on top of him!

Rocky looked at Archie and grinned.
"At least we know the swing works!"

The vine swung back to Mazu. "Do you want to go next, Bill?" she asked.

Bill shook his head. "I'm going to stay right here where it's safe," he said.

But it WASN'T safe. From nearby, they head a mighty ROAR. Mazu, Bill and Tiny were on the same side of the crevice as GIGANTO! The only way to escape was over the gap.

Bill quickly changed his mind about the swing. He grabbed hold of the vine and leapt into the air, but instead of flying across, he was left dangling in the crevice.

Tiny came to the rescue. Using her Triceratops strength, she grabbed the other end of the vine and heaved Bill out again.

Bill was very glad to be back on solid ground, but the friends still needed to find a way across. Luckily, Giganto seemed to have lost interest in the little dinos and had stomped towards the geysers.

Mazu spotted Archie on the other side and another idea sprang to mind. "That's it!" she gasped. "We can FLY over!"

Tiny wasn't so sure. Archie HADN'T flown – he had been blasted over by a geyser!

A minute later, Bill looked up to see Mazu sitting proudly on top of a homemade catapult. She had tied the end of a palm tree to a rock with a vine, and once the rock was pushed aside, Mazu would be flung across the gap.

Mazu was ready for lift-off. Tiny pushed the rock away and — PINNNGG! — the tree was released, flinging the little Ankylosaurus into the air.

And we have a perfect launch!

She sailed over the crevice. Just like Rocky she had a nice soft landing — right on top of Archie!

Archie rubbed his head. "How do I manage to crash when I'm not the one flying?"

Mazu got back to her feet. Now only Tiny and Bill were left to cross.

Tiny took Bill's hands. It was okay to be scared. They were ALL scared!

"As long as I have my friends around to help me, I know I'll be all right," she said. "How about we go together?"

Bill beamed at her. Now he felt much better.

Bill climbed onto the Dino Launcher 3000, while Tiny hurried round to move the rock. Archie, Mazu and Rocky watched nervously from the other side.

"WATCH OUT!" shouted Archie from his tree. He, Mazu and Rocky had spotted . . .

Giganto stomped towards the Dino Launcher 3000 and bent down to take a look. His huge tail swung towards Tiny and pinned her to the rock. She was stuck!

"Bill!" Tiny called. "If you cut the vine, you can escape! I'll find a way across later."

But even though he was still shaking with fear, there was no way Bill was leaving his friend behind.

Bill caught sight of the hot spring and had a brilliant idea.
It was time for him to be brave.

"Hey, Giganto!" he shouted, jumping into a geyser.

Bill stirred up the bubbles, just like Mazu had done earlier. Sure enough,
a jet of water erupted into the air. Forgetting about the little dinos,
Giganto stepped into the springs to enjoy a hot shower.

Bill rushed back to the Dino Launcher 3000, and together he and Tiny climbed up onto it. Tiny tried to cut the vine to release the trunk – but it was too tough!

They heard a single loud STOMP and looked up to see GIGANTO! The little dinos cowered as he loomed over them – but then he sniffed the air and turned away.

"Is he going to leave us alone?" Bill said hopefully.

As Giganto walked away, his tail knocked the rock off the vine. The Dino Launcher 3000 was finally released and Bill and Tiny glided through the air.

Now it was their turn to crash-land on top of poor Archie!

"You were really brave, Bill," Tiny said as she leapt to her feet. "I'm so proud of you!"

"I was so worried about you, I forgot to be worried about myself," Bill said. "And you know what? It felt great!"

Now he knew there was no need to be afraid when his friends were around him.

When the little dinosaurs got home, everyone was talking about Bill's great adventure.

"You should have seen Bill stir up that geyser right in front of Giganto," said Rocky. "He was so brave!"

"We learnt something new about Giganto, too," said Mazu. "Now we know that he likes to take baths in the geysers!"

Bill decided to try a geyser shower too. But when he jumped in – WHOOSH! – the jet of water was much too high for him.

"Geysers aren't fun at all!" Bill wailed. "Someone get me down!"

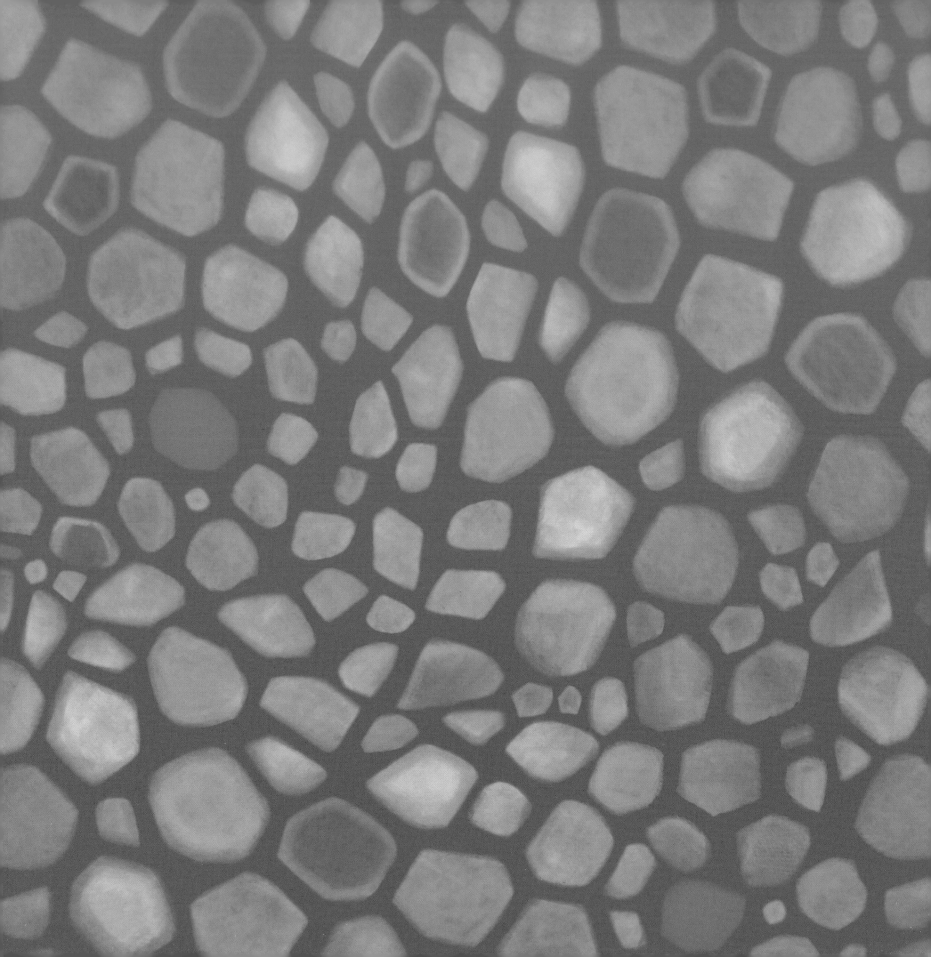

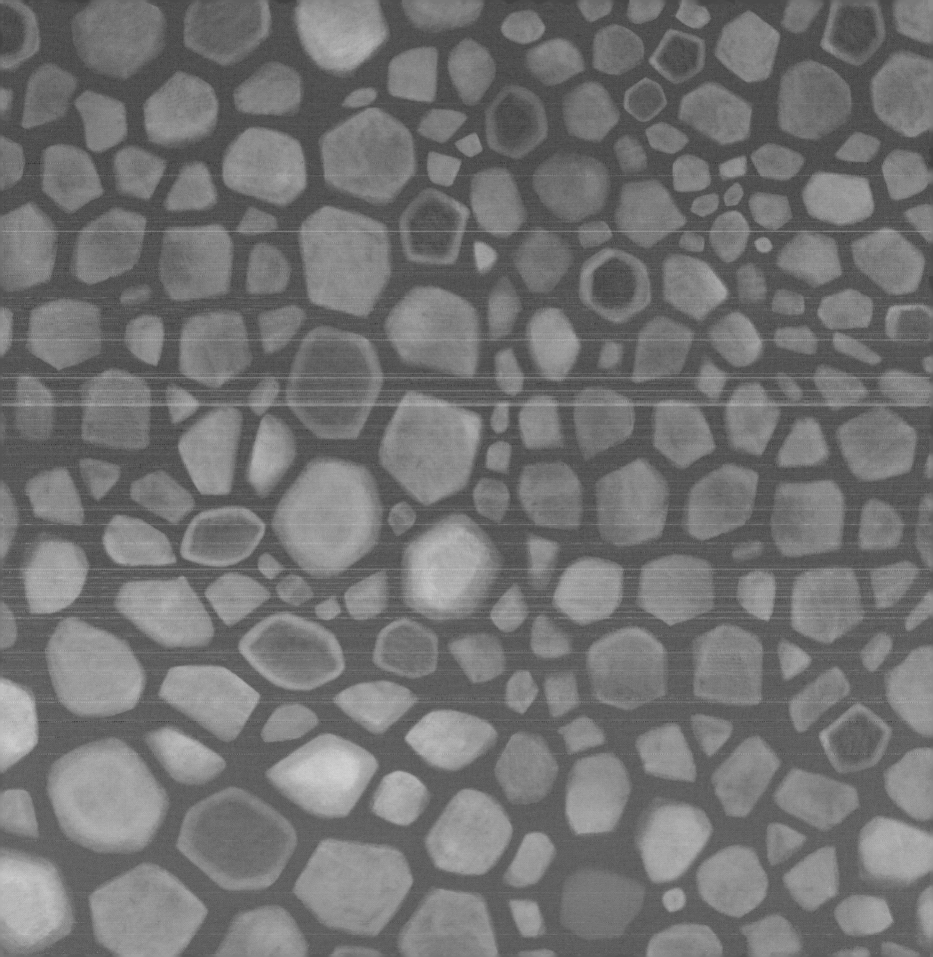

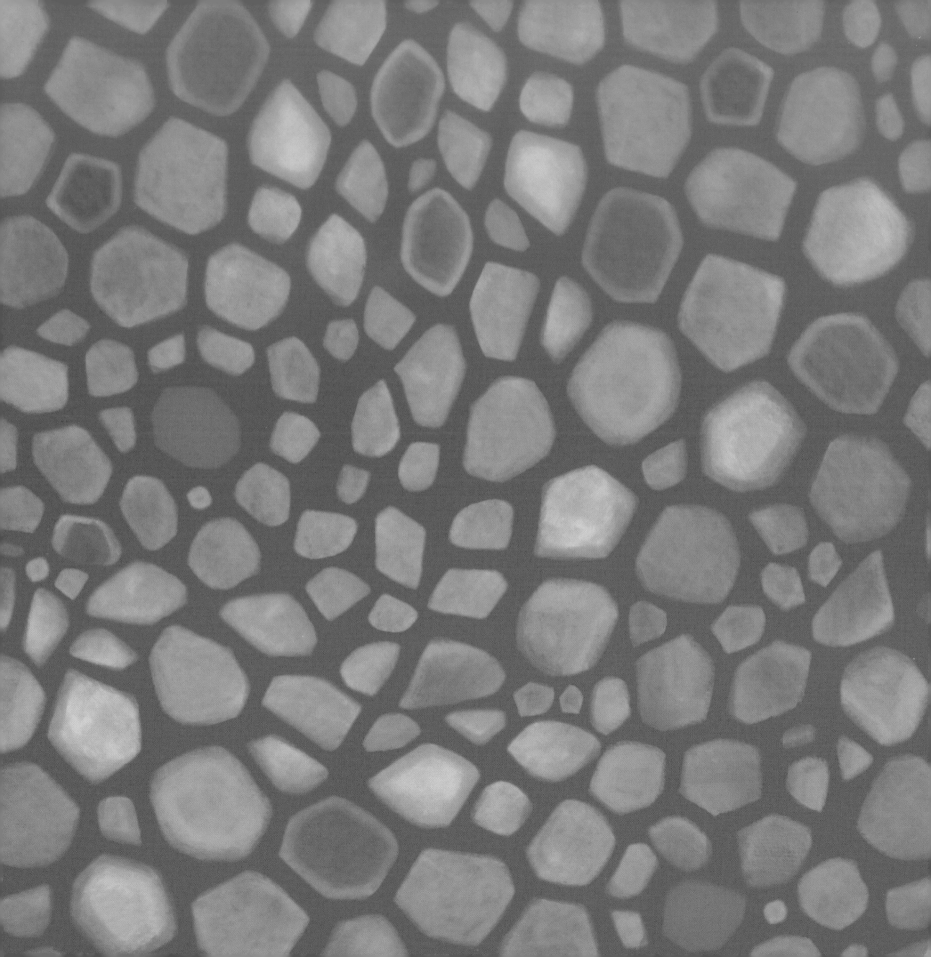